THE IRON STONES

By Danny Pearson
& Steve Beckett

TITLES IN THE STRANGE TOWN SET
BIGFOOT RESCUE
THE SPACE KITTEN
SHOPPING SPREE
THOR NEXT DOOR
THE IRON STONES
EXTRA TIME
RUBBISH INVASION
GOING UNDERGROUND

Badger Publishing Limited
Oldmedow Road,
Hardwick Industrial Estate,
King's Lynn PE30 4JJ

Telephone: 01438 791037
www.badgerlearning.co.uk

2 4 6 8 10 9 7 5 3 1

The Iron Stones
ISBN 978-1-78464-689-9

Text © Danny Pearson 2017
Complete work © Badger Publishing Limited 2017

Publisher: Susan Ross
Senior Editor: Danny Pearson
Series Consultant: Tim Collins
Illustration: Steve Beckett
Designer: Fiona Grant

THE IRON STONES

CONTENTS

Logan is not exactly happy about having to move to a town in the middle of nowhere. It looks funny, it smells funny and it even feels funny, if that's possible?

Everyone, and everything, in this town just doesn't seem right, but no one seems to care or even notice. Everyone, that is, apart from Eva. She has spent years collecting evidence of the weird goings-on in Strange Town.

Eva, Logan and his dog, Otis, are the Strange Town Squad – always ready and on the look out for all things odd.

You are about to find out that some towns can be stranger than others.

Welcome to Strange Town.

CAST OF CHARACTERS

Logan

Eva

Otis

The Iron Stones

VOCABULARY

addicted   imaginary
embarrassing   security
generation   unbelievable

Chapter One

Sold Out

Logan's dad came running into the kitchen with a huge grin on his face. "The Iron Stones are coming to town and guess who has tickets to both of their sold-out shows?" he said, tapping his shirt pocket.

Logan held his head in his hands. "Oh, no. They aren't that silly band you used to like when you were younger? That metal band that sounds like a herd of elephants with colds?"

"I'll have you know that they do not sound like a herd of sick elephants. They are the finest band in the world!" his dad said as he dusted off a record and placed it on the player.

"Here son, listen to this."

RAAAAAAA!!!

"Aaargh, turn that off!" Logan yelled, covering his ears. "It's so embarrassing!"

His dad turned it up even louder and started waving his arms about as if he was playing a guitar. "No taste in music at all. Your generation is addicted to bubble-gum boybands and beats made by a computer. Real bands use guitars and drum kits."

Logan rolled his eyes back. "Sure Dad, whatever you say."

There was a knock at the door.

Logan's mum went to answer it. "Hello Eva. Please come in. You are just in time to be taught a lesson in what great music is … apparently."

"YEAH! I love this one!" she yelled. "Turn it up, turn it up!"

Logan looked at his friend and his dad leaping around and playing imaginary guitars. He winced. Why couldn't they see how crazy they looked?

Chapter Two

Older

Eva insisted on staying at Logan's house until his dad returned from the gig. She wanted to hear every last detail.

"Apparently they look and sound better now than they ever have," she said. "I am so jealous your dad managed to get tickets to see them on both nights."

Logan folded his arms. "I don't get why you like them so much. It's sad going to watch a bunch of old men run about on stage."

"OK," Eva replied. "They may be old, but look at them. I hope I end up looking and feeling that good at seventy."

"Seventy!" Logan spluttered.

They could hear a key in the door.

Eva leaped up like she was on a giant spring. "It must be your dad. Let's see how it went."

Logan's dad stumbled in. He looked shattered. In the few hours he'd been out of the house his hair had become greyer.

Otis ran up to give him a welcome lick but screeched to a halt as soon as he saw his face. He turned around and ran back to his dog bed, yelping.

YELP! YELP!

"WOW! Someone really rocked out. How was it?" asked Eva.

Logan's dad slowly punched the air with one fist. "It was awesome!" Then he slumped into a chair. "But now I think it's time for sleep."

"Oh dear, I don't think you can handle these late nights," Logan's mum said. "You aren't as young as you used to be."

She pushed him towards the stairs. "If you want any chance of making it to tomorrow's gig then you need your beauty sleep. You look ten years older than you did before you went."

Logan nudged Eva. "He does, you know. He looks ten years older. He didn't have grey hair earlier."

"What are you thinking?" Eva asked.

"I'm thinking something is going on at those Iron Stones gigs. There's no way a band can be in their seventies and still run around like teenagers. Something doesn't add up," said Logan.

A smile appeared on Eva's face. "So are we going down to the Iron Stones gig tomorrow?"

Logan looked at her. "As painful as it may be, yes. Yes we are."

"YES!" Eva dropped to her knees and slid down the corridor, pretending to play the guitar.

Chapter Three

Backstage

Logan watched his dad handing his ticket over to a huge man wearing a blue jacket. He still looked very old and very tired. Catching up on sleep hadn't helped him at all.

"There is no way we are going to get in without tickets. Any ideas?" asked Logan.

"Of course," Eva replied. "I know a back way in. My dad used to work here."

"A back way? Past all the backstage security?" asked Logan shaking his head. "That is the most idiotic idea you have ever had." But it was too late. Eva was running round the back of the building.

2 MINUTES LATER...

Eva gave Otis a rub behind his ear. "OK, Otis. You bark and run rings round that security guard to distract him while we sneak in. Got it?"

Otis raised his head, puffed out his chest and gave out a short, sharp yap.

He ran over to the security guard and barked as loudly as he could.

BARK!

"Get out of here!" shouted the security guard. "You shouldn't be here."

Otis lifted a leg to pee on him.

"That's it!" yelled the guard. "No one wees on me!"

Otis scampered away and the guard ran after him.

BARK! BARK! BARK!

Eva and Logan quickly made their way through the door. They wandered down a long corridor and past the back of a huge speaker until they came to a thick, black curtain. Through a gap at the end of it they could see the Iron Stones on stage.

Logan popped ear plugs into his ears. "Not for me, thanks."

Eva watched them from behind the curtain. "These guys are even better live. You don't know what you're missing out on."

The whole building was shaking from the loud music.

"Sorry, can't hear you," Logan said pointing to his ears. "I'm off to have a look around to see if these guys are up to something."

1 HOUR LATER...

Logan had looked all over the backstage area but couldn't see anything.

The band were coming off stage. He pressed himself against the wall and removed his ear plugs.

The tall lead singer bent over to a tap that was sticking out of the back of the large speaker. He filled up his cup with a weird-looking green liquid.

"Cheers to the fans of Strange Town for giving us the energy we need," he laughed as he drank the green drink in one go.

The drummer also took a cup and filled it from the tap. "And cheers to this little beauty for sucking in their youth so we can rock on forever!"

The band all laughed as they filled their cups from the speaker tap.

"Quick, boys, we are back on," cried the lead singer. "Let's give them a show they will never forget."

"That's it!" Logan said. "They are somehow draining life and energy from their fans through that speaker. I have to warn Eva."

Chapter Four

Final Encore

Eva was still staring through the gap in the curtains.

Logan grabbed her shoulders and span her round. She looked older and more drained than she had done just an hour earlier.

"I know what is going on!" said Logan. "They are literally sucking the life out of people."

"I know you don't like their music but that's a bit harsh," Eva said.

"No! Look," Logan said, pointing down the corridor, "that speaker is sucking in energy from the fans in the crowd. From you. From whoever is listening to their music in here."

Eva looked confused. "What? No, they wouldn't."

"See for yourself," said Logan, pointing to a mirror on the wall behind them. "They are draining the life out of you and using it for themselves. How do you think they have stayed so young for all these years?"

"**AAARGH!**" Eva screamed as she looked into the mirror. "We need to stop them. Strange Town Squad to the rescue!"

Logan handed Eva a set of ear plugs. "Quick! Put these in before they start the encore."

He spotted a man with grey hair in the middle of the crowd. It took Logan a few moments to recognise his dad.

"It looks like we're running out of time," he said. "We'd better be quick."

The security guard was stomping down the corridor towards them.

"Oi!" he shouted. "What are you doing back here? Been snooping around have we?" he said as he dragged them back. "Well we don't want you kids letting people know about the band's little secret, now do we?"

YAP! YAP! YAP!

Otis came rushing towards them.

"Ha! Good boy," said Logan. He pointed at the speaker. "Go jump on that and knock it over."

Otis's ears stood up and he turned to face the giant speaker. He moved his stumpy little sausage legs as fast as he could and hurled himself against it.

The speaker swung back and forth like a rocking horse and then crashed forwards onto the stage.

"Oops," said the security guard, letting go of Eva and Logan. "Looks like the show is over."

Eva and Logan peered through the curtain again.

Green energy was shooting out of the broken speaker in all directions. Straight back into the fans and out of the front door.

The band looked at each other in horror. They had all aged by about fifty years.

"Quick, run!" shouted the lead singer. He ran his hands through his hair and huge clumps of it fell out.

They hobbled out of the back door, clutching their backs and their hips.

As soon as they were in the tour bus it screeched away at high speed.

VROOOOOOM!

The crowd roared!

ROAR!

None of them could remember seeing stage effects like that before.

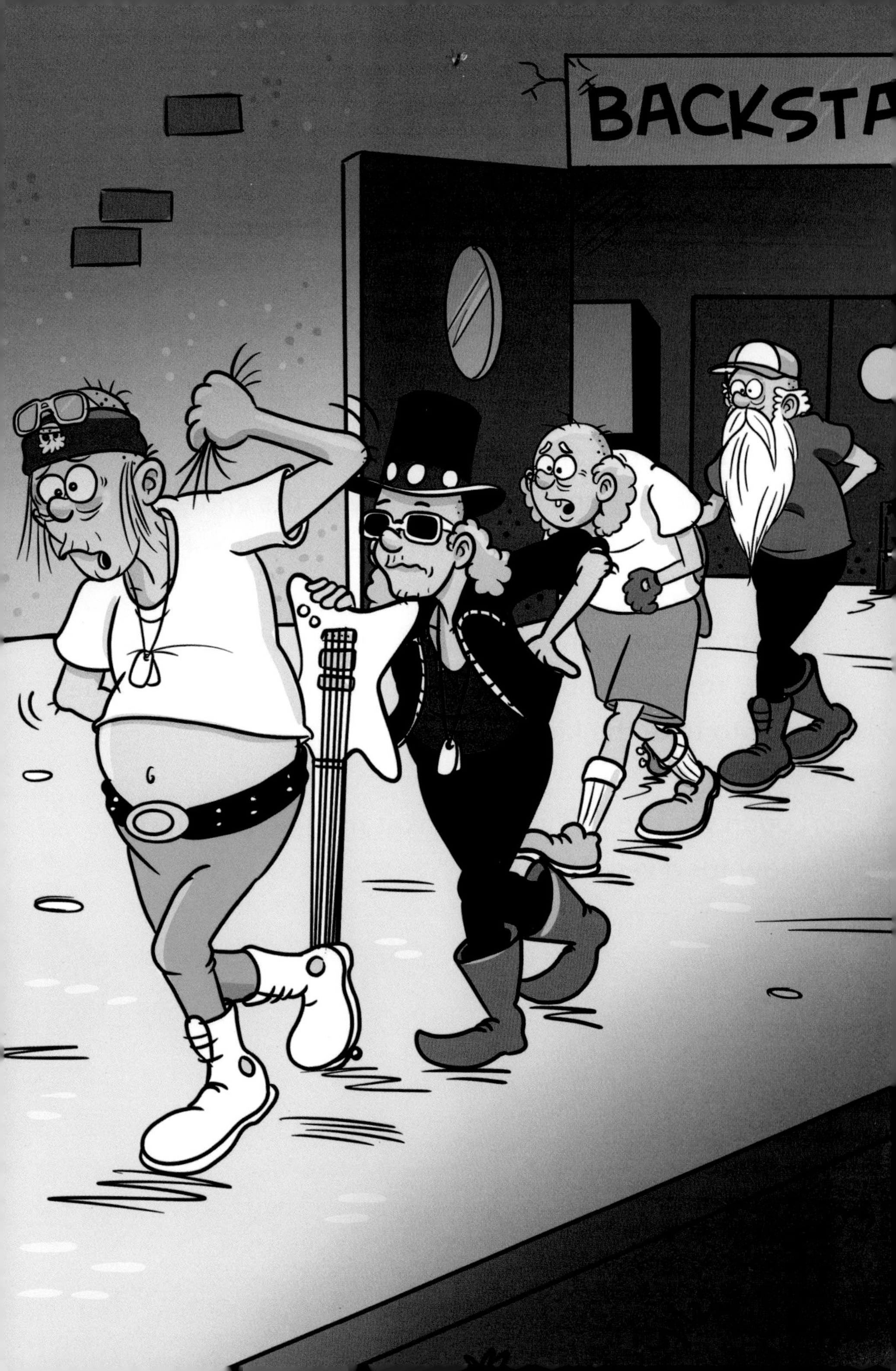
BACKSTA

LATER THAT NIGHT...

Logan and Eva were sitting back in the kitchen. They had just made it back before his dad arrived home.

"How was it?" asked Eva.

"Amazing," he said, jumping into the air. "They sounded great and the light show at the end was unbelievable. Best show ever! They've still got it!"

Logan's mum came in. "Wow! There is my handsome man. You look much better. Maybe next time you'll be able to take the kids along?"

Logan winked at Eva. "I think it may be their last show for a very long time."

QUESTIONS

1. What was Logan's dad so happy about?
   (page 6)

2. What did Otis do after Logan's dad walked through the door? *(page 12)*

3. How did Logan and Eva get into the concert building? *(pages 16-17)*

4. How did the band stay so young? *(page 19)*

5. Who knocked over the giant speaker? *(page 23)*

6. What is your favourite band or singer?

MEET THE
AUTHOR AND ILLUSTRATOR

THE AUTHOR

Danny Pearson landed on
planet Earth during the 1980s.
He assures us that the
Strange Town series is based
on actual events that have
happened in the strange town
that he lives in.

THE ILLUSTRATOR

Steve Beckett has a robot arm
that is programmed to draw
funny pictures. He likes
playing with toy soldiers
and dreams of being an ace
survival expert. He is scared
of heights, creepy crawlies and
doesn't like camping!